Dogbird

Paul Stewart

Illustrated by
Tony Ross

CORGI PUPS

www.**books**at**transworld**.co.uk/childrens

For Anna

Series Reading Consultant: Prue Goodwin
Reading and Language Information Centre,
University of Reading

DOGBIRD
A CORGI PUPS BOOK : 0 552 546011

First publication in Great Britain

PRINTING HISTORY
Corgi Pups edition published 1998

7 9 10 8 6

Set in Bembo Schoolbook

Corgi Books are published by Transworld Publishers,
61–63 Uxbridge Road, London W5 5SA,
a division of The Random House Group Ltd,
in Australia by Random House Australia (Pty) Ltd,
20 Alfred Street, Milsons Point, Sydney, NSW 2061,
in New Zealand by Random House New Zealand Ltd,
18 Poland Road, Glenfield, Auckland 10,
and in South Africa by Random House (Pty) Ltd,
Endulini, 5a Jubilee Road, Parktown 2193.

Made and printed in Great Britain by
Cox & Wyman Ltd, Reading, Berkshire.

Contents

Chapter One

It was lunchtime. Alice Carey
was sitting at the table with her
mum and dad. The radio was
on, but the music was drowned
out by the sound of howling.

"That wretched bird is driving me round the bend!" Dad muttered.

At that moment the door burst open, and Lex, Lol and Lance – the family's three black labradors – bounded into the room and barked up at the birdcage.

Alice's mum jumped up. As she did so, the table-cloth got caught round her leg, and the whole lot – plates of lasagne, glasses of water and orange squash, knives and forks, salt and pepper – came crashing to the floor.

"That's it!" her dad stormed.
"That bird has got to go!"

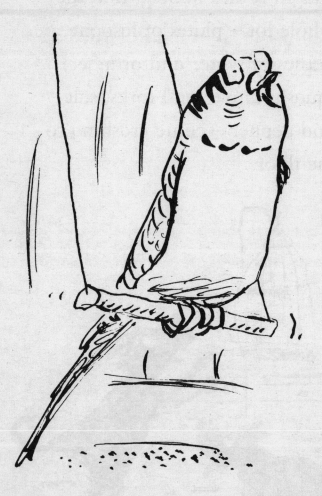

The bird in question was a budgie. He belonged to Alice.

On her seventh birthday, her mum and dad had taken her to the pet-shop to choose her very own pet. But what animal would be best?

With Lex, Lol and Lance
around, it wouldn't be fair to
buy a kitten.

And Alice thought that guinea
pigs were boring.

And Alice's mum refused to
have a snake in the house!

So it was that, after much
humming and haaing, Alice
chose a budgie.

"Perfect," said Mum.

"Ideal," said Dad.

It was only later that they
discovered how wrong they had
both been.

The pet-shop man told them
the budgie was a talker. On the
way home, Alice sat in the car
with the cage on her lap. She
tried to teach him a couple of
things. "*Who's a clever boy,
then?*" and "*My name's Blue.*"

But by the time they pulled
up outside Alice's house, the
budgie hadn't said a single word.

"Wait till we get him inside,"
said Mum. "He'll soon find his
voice then."

Mum turned the key in the lock and pushed the door open. Lex, Lol and Lance raced into the hallway. Normally, they were quiet, but the sight and smell of the bright blue bird seemed to drive them crazy.

Time and again they jumped
up at the cage, barking
furiously.

And the budgie? Well, Alice's
mum was right. He did find his
voice. He opened his beak and
barked back at them.

"Dogbird," Dad laughed –
and the name stuck.

From that moment on, life in
the Carey family changed – and
for the worse. For although it
seemed funny at first, a barking
budgie was no joke.

Dogbird barked at the milkman.
He barked at the postman.

He barked when Alice's friends
came to play. And every time
he barked, Lex, Lol and Lance
would join in. It drove everyone
bonkers.

Woof! Woof! Woof!

Louder and louder, they
would get. The budgie and the
dogs, all barking wildly together.
Once they'd started nothing
would make them stop.

Woof! Woof! Woof!

Sometimes the dogs would escape from the kitchen into the sitting-room where Dogbird's cage hung by the window. It was then that the barking grew loudest of all. You couldn't hear yourself think.

WOOF! WOOF! WOOF! WOOF!

Day after day, the barking would start up. Night after night, everyone's sleep was disturbed. The neighbours complained. Someone wrote to the council.

Now, six weeks later, with the dogs jumping around in the remains of their lunch and Dogbird still loudly barking, Alice's dad had finally reached the end of his tether.

Chapter Two

Before Alice could protest, the
telephone rang. It was Grandma
and, from the look on her mum's
face, something was wrong.

"Oh, how awful," she said. "Stay where you are. We'll be right over." She put the phone down. "Grandma's been burgled."

Alice shuddered. "Poor Grandma," she said. "She'll want one of my special cuddles."

"No, Alice. Not now," said
her mum. "Grandma sounded in
rather a state. You can play
with Katie while we go and see
how she is."

"We'll be seeing her again
tomorrow," said Dad. "You can
cuddle her then."

Alice knew there was no point arguing – at least they'd forgotten about Dogbird. At that moment, though, Lex, Lol and Lance came tearing back into the room to remind them. Their wagging tails sent everything flying. The barking was deafening!

"Not again!" Mum shouted. "Get to your baskets, the lot of you!"

"I'll tell you what," said Dad, as he grabbed the dogs by their collars. "*We'd* never get burgled. A loud dog is better than any alarm."

"And we've got three!" said
Mum.

Dogbird growled. Alice stared
at him sadly.

"Four," she said quietly.

Katie was Alice's best friend and
next-door neighbour. As they sat
together in Katie's tree-house,
Alice told her all about the
burglars.

"They took *everything!*" she
said.

"Everything?" gasped Katie.

"All Grandma's secret treasures," Alice said. She was enjoying the look of wide-eyed horror on her friend's face. "Of course," she said, "*we'd* never get burgled – because of the dogs."

Katie nodded. "I wish we had a dog," she said. "Dad says

they're too much trouble. And too noisy."

"But it's the noise that's important," said Alice. "The barking frightens the burglars away..."

As she spoke, the noise in question – barking – exploded from Alice's house. It was Lex, Lol, Lance and, loudest of all, Dogbird.

Katie spun round. "Burglars!" she cried.

But Alice didn't think so.
"Quick!" she cried. "Before
we're too late!"

Chapter Three

The two girls leapt down from
the tree-house, slipped through
the hole in the fence, and raced
to the back of Alice's house.

They peered in through the
window. Alice saw the dogs
leaping about, the cage on its
side – the flapping wings.

"DOGBIRD!" she screamed.
She hammered on the glass,
but the dogs took no notice.
Their game was far too much
fun.

Alice dashed to the back door, through the kitchen and into the sitting-room. When she got there, things had gone from bad to worse.

The cage door had sprung open and Dogbird was now free. He was fluttering between

the lights and the picture-rail,
with the dogs crashing about
after him.

They knocked over the coffee
table, they leapt on the settee,
they scrabbled up the wall
shelves. Books tumbled, cushions
flew. There was millet everywhere.

Crash!

Mum's favourite vase lay in pieces on the floor.

"GET TO YOUR BASKETS," Alice bellowed.

The dogs froze. The game was clearly over. Heads down and tails between their legs, they plodded back to the kitchen.

Alice slammed the door behind
them and hurried to Dogbird.

Katie had stood the cage up,
and Dogbird was back inside,
trembling.

"Poor thing," said Alice. "Did the naughty doggies frighten you?" She turned to Katie. "It's been like this ever since I got him."

"I know," said Katie. "I live next door, remember."

"Is it *really* noisy?" Alice asked.

"Sometimes," said Katie. "It makes Dad so grumpy."

"I'm sorry," said Alice.
"It's the dogs – they won't leave him alone."

Katie shrugged. "Perhaps it's not their fault."

"What do you mean?" said Alice.

"Well," she said. "What do you think a dog says when it barks?"

Alice laughed. "*Hello*, I suppose."

"Or, *Go away! I'm dangerous!*" said Katie.

"Or, *Let's play!*" said Alice.

"Exactly!" said Katie.
"And those are the things that
Dogbird is saying to them when
he barks. The dogs are only
responding. They're probably
just trying to get him out of the
cage so they can go and play."

Alice nodded. It made sense.
Trust her to end up with a
budgie that could only speak
dog.

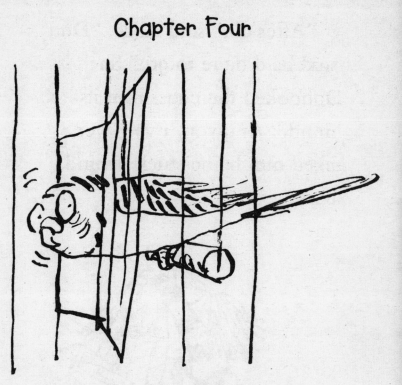

Chapter Four

Afterwards, neither Alice nor
Katie could remember who first
suggested setting Dogbird free.
The idea just sort of happened,
the way ideas sometimes do.

"After all," said Alice, "Dad said he'd have to go." She unhooked the cage from its stand. "Anyway, I've never liked him being stuck behind bars."

"He must get lonely on his
own," said Katie. She followed
her friend across the room. "In
Australia, the wild ones live in
flocks."

Alice sighed. "All Dogbird's got is his reflection."

She opened the French windows and stepped outside. Dogbird wagged his tail feathers.

"He can hear the call of the wild," Katie whispered.

"A bird needs to be free," said Alice. She opened the cage door. Dogbird didn't move. "I said ... Dogbird! Get out of there."

Dogbird hopped to the end of
the perch, and watched Alice
through one mistrustful eye.
Alice reached inside the cage.
Dogbird growled and snapped at
her fingers.

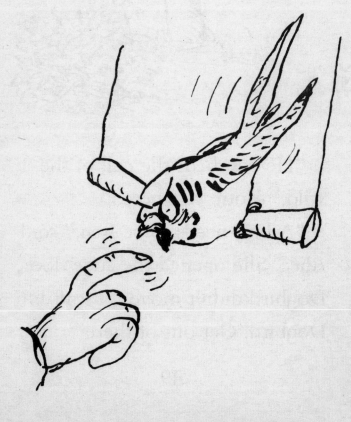

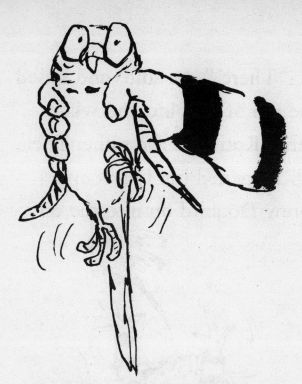

But Alice would not be put
off. She had decided to set
Dogbird free, and that was what
she was going to do. Quickly
and gently, she closed her hand
around his body, and pulled him
from the cage.

"There," she said, and kissed
the top of his blue and white
head. Katie did the same. Then
Alice opened her hands and
threw Dogbird up into the air.

"*Woof!*" said Dogbird, and
soared off into the sunset – a
flash of sky-blue.

"He did it!" Katie shouted
excitedly.

Alice nodded. There was a
lump in her throat. "Bye-bye,
Dogbird," she whispered. "Be
happy!"

They were stepping back into
the house when a sudden noise

filled the air. Horrible it was! A stomach-churning screeching and squawking and jabbering – and above it all, the sound of frenzied barking.

"Look!" Katie cried, but Alice had already seen.

High above the treetops, Dogbird was being attacked. There were sparrows, starlings, blackbirds, magpies, crows – all ganging up on the sky-blue intruder.

"Leave him alone!" Alice screamed.

But it was no good. The birds wouldn't rest until they had driven Dogbird away. Or worse!

"It's all gone wrong," Alice wailed, as Dogbird darted this way and that, trying to avoid the sharp beaks and claws.

"Dogbird!" she called. "Come back!"

As if only waiting to be asked, Dogbird barked, twisted round in mid-air and swooped down towards her. The flock of furious birds followed close behind.

"Faster," yelled Katie.

Alice stretched out her arm. Dogbird flew closer, barking all the while – and landed. The other birds flew off and chattered angrily from the tree and fence. Dogbird shivered miserably. There were spots of blood on his wing.

"Now what?" said Alice sadly. She hung the cage back on its stand.

Katie shrugged. Dogbird barked. And both girls heard the sound of the key in the lock.

"Hello?" said Dad, surprised.
"What are you two doing
here?"

"And what's all this mess?"
Mum demanded.

"It was the dogs," Alice
explained. "They knocked the
bird-cage over." Dad groaned.

Then, not wanting to tell them about trying to set Dogbird free, she asked, "How's Grandma?"

"Fine," said Mum. "But a bit worried the burglars might come back."

"She should get a dog," said Dad. "She'd feel much safer."

"She couldn't cope," said Mum. "The walks, the feeds ..."

Alice and Katie looked at one another and grinned. That was it! That was the answer.

"What if I gave her
Dogbird?" said Alice.

Mum smiled. "Perfect!" she
said.

"Ideal!" said Dad.

And this time, they were right.

★ ★ ★

And so it was that Dogbird went
to live with Grandma. Life in
the Carey household changed
again – this time for the better.

The dogs stopped barking.

The neighbours stopped complaining. And everyone finally got a good night's sleep.

As for Grandma, she was overjoyed with the budgie. He kept her company and was no trouble at all. She called him Bluey.

Alice often went to see the pair of them. She was pleased to see that the bird was happy at last. Grandma kept the cage door open so that Bluey could fly in and out as he pleased. He never tried to escape – even when the windows were open.

And being with Grandma, he soon learned to speak.

"Pretty Bluey," he would say. And sometimes, *"Now where have I put my glasses?"*

Best of all, he made Grandma
feel safe. Whenever the gate
clicked, or the doorbell rang, or
he heard someone prowling
around outside, Bluey would
become Dogbird again, and
bark and bark and bark.